# A Note to Parents

### Read to your child...

★ Reading aloud is one of the best ways to develop your child's love of reading. Read together at least 20 minutes each day.

★ Enthusiasm is contagious! Read with feeling. Show your child that reading is fun.

★ Take time to answer questions your child may have about the story. Linger over pages that interest your child.

### ...and your child will read to you.

★ Follow cues from your child to know when he wants to join in the reading.

★ Support your young reader. Give him a word whenever he asks for it.

★ Praise your child as he progresses. Your encouraging words will build his confidence.

### You can help your Level 1 reader.

★ Reading begins with knowing how a book works. Show your child the title and where the story begins.

★ Ask your child to find picture clues on each page. Talk about what is happening in the story.

★ Point to the words as you read so your child can make the connection between the print and the story.

★ Ask your child to point to words she knows.

★ Let your child supply the rhyming words.

*Most of all, enjoy your reading time together!*

**—Bernice Cullinan, Ph.D.,**
**Professor of Reading, New York University**

Published by Reader's Digest Children's Books
Reader's Digest Road, Pleasantville, NY U.S.A. 10570-7000 and
Reader's Digest Children's Publishing Limited,
The Ice House, 124-126 Walcot Street, Bath UK BA1 5BG
Text copyright © 2006 Reader's Digest Children's Publishing, Inc.
All rights reserved. Reader's Digest Children's Books is a trademark and
Reader's Digest is a registered trademark of The Reader's Digest Association, Inc.
Manufactured in China.
Conforms to ASTM F963 and EN 71
10 9 8 7 6 5 4 3 2 1

Library of Congress Cataloging-in-Publication Data

Herman, Gail, 1959–
Under construction / written by Gail Herman.
    p. cm. – (All-star readers. Level 1)
"Tonka."
    ISBN-13: 978-0-7944-1001-8
    ISBN- 10: 0-7944-1001-4
I. Title. II. Series.

PZ7.H4315Un 2006            2005044351

# Under Construction

by Gail Herman
illustrated by Thomas LaPadula

**1**

All-Star Readers™

**Reader's Digest Children's Books™**

Pleasantville, New York • Montréal, Québec

We are moving into a
new house.

A brand-new house.
It has just been built.

The house is nice. But I feel sad.
It is far from all my friends.

"Look, Robby!" says Dad. "Look next door!"

I see a big old house.
"So what? Who wants to live
near that?" I say.

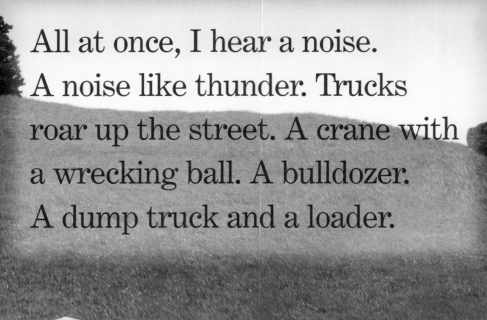

All at once, I hear a noise.
A noise like thunder. Trucks
roar up the street. A crane with
a wrecking ball. A bulldozer.
A dump truck and a loader.

"Dad, I can watch the trucks," says Robby. "I can watch them work."

*Boom! Crash!* The wrecking ball swings. It's tearing down the old house!

Walls crack. Bricks tumble. What a mess!

*Clank, clank!* The bulldozer pushes. The loader scoops.

I watch the trucks.
I watch them work.

The dump truck rumbles over.
In goes the mess!

Now what is next
door? There's a great big
hole! But soon, new
trucks come along.

Each day I watch the trucks.
Each day I watch them work.

A cement mixer whirrs and whirrs. Its giant drum turns.

Concrete pours out. "That is the foundation," Dad says. "Everything else goes on top."

Trucks bring more supplies—
heavy round pipes and stacks
of wood and bricks.

Each week I watch the trucks.
Each week I watch them work.

I see a crane lift up a section of the house.

Up to the top it goes!

"This is a new house," says Dad.
"It takes a lot of time."

Each week I watch the trucks.
Each week I watch them work.
At last! The building is done!

One by one, the trucks drive off.
"Now what?" I ask.

"What will I do with nothing to watch and no one to play with?"

Hey! Here come more trucks. They are moving trucks, bringing a new family! They're bringing new friends to play with. Hooray!

# Color in the star next to each word you can read.

☆ are
☆ ball
☆ been
☆ built
☆ crack
☆ crane
☆ door
☆ down
☆ drive
☆ drum
☆ dump
☆ each
☆ far
☆ feel
☆ goes
☆ great
☆ hole

☆ house
☆ just
☆ lift
☆ live
☆ look
☆ mess
☆ mixer
☆ moving
☆ near
☆ new
☆ next
☆ nice
☆ noise
☆ off
☆ once
☆ out
☆ over

☆ pipes
☆ play
☆ round
☆ sad
☆ scoops
☆ see
☆ soon
☆ street
☆ top
☆ trucks
☆ walls
☆ wants
☆ we
☆ what
☆ who
☆ wood
☆ work